Every new generation of children is enthralled by the famous stories in our Well-loved Tales series. Younger ones love to have the story read to them. Older children will enjoy the exciting stories in an easy-to-read text.

Published by Ladybird Books Ltd Loughborough Leicestershire UK
Ladybird Books Inc Lewiston Maine 04240 USA

WELL-LOVED TALES

The Goose Girl

HARRISON DISTRICT 2
STRATTON MEADOWS

retold for easy reading
by JOAN COLLINS

illustrated by KATHIE LAYFIELD

Ladybird Books

Once upon a time, there was a beautiful princess. She lived with her mother, the queen, in a castle on a hill.

Her father, the king, died when the princess was a baby. When she grew up, she was going to marry a prince who lived in a far away country.

One day, the queen said to her, "You are old enough to leave me and go to marry your prince."

The princess was sad to leave her mother for they loved each other very much.

She packed up all her pretty dresses and
fine jewels, and the queen gave her some
wonderful presents.

The present the princess liked most was
a white horse that could talk. His name
was Falada.

When the time came to say goodbye,
the queen cut off a lock of her hair. She
gave it to the princess, saying, "Take this,
my dear daughter. It's a charm to keep
you safe."

The princess tucked it carefully into the top of her dress. The queen gave her one last present.

"Here is a golden cup," she said. "You can drink out of it when you come to a river."

Then the princess set off, with her maid, on their long journey.

As they rode along, over hills and through woods, the princess began to feel thirsty.

"O my maid," she said, "please take my golden cup and fetch me some water from the river."

"Fetch it yourself!" said the maid in a nasty voice. "Why should I take orders from you?" She was jealous of the princess.

The princess did not want to make a fuss. So she knelt down on the river bank to reach the water. But the lock of hair

fell out of her dress and floated away
down the river.

"Alas!" said the princess. "I have lost
the charm my mother gave me!"

The maid was pleased. Now the charm
was lost, the princess was in her power.

"Take off your fine clothes," she said,
"and give them to me. You can wear these
old rags."

Poor princess! No one had ever been
unkind to her before. She humbly did as
she was told.

Now the maid rode on Falada, wearing the princess's dress. The princess rode on the maid's horse, in rags and tatters.

At last they reached the prince's palace.

"If you tell a living person who you really are," said the wicked maid, "I will kill you! You must promise to tell

nobody, by the sky above.'' The princess
was so frightened that she promised.

The old king and his son the young
prince came out to welcome them. They
both thought the maid was the princess,

because of her fine clothes. They took her inside the palace, while the real princess had to stand outside, in the cold.

The king looked out of the window and saw her. "Who is that lovely girl in rags and tatters?" he asked the maid.

"Just a poor beggar I met on the way. Could you give her some work to do?" asked the maid.

"She can help Curdken to look after the geese," said the old king, who was sorry for her.

"I would like you to do something for *me*," said the maid boldly.

"What is that?" asked the king.

"Have the horse I rode on killed. He behaved very badly on the way," said the maid. She was afraid Falada would speak and give away her secret.

The king sent a servant to take Falada away. The princess ran after him, crying, but she could not save the talking horse. So she gave the man a gold coin and asked him to fasten the horse's head high up on the city gate. Then she would be able to see her old friend each time she took the geese out into the fields.

The first morning as she went through the gate, she looked up at him sadly, and said:

> "Falada, poor Falada, hanging up
> there!"

The magic horse answered her:

> "Princess, poor princess, passing
> down there!
> Alas, alas, if your mother knew,
> How sad her heart would be for
> you!"

Curdken was the boy who looked after the geese. He liked to tease the girls and pull their hair and pinch them.

The princess had beautiful, long, fair hair. She kept it hidden under a scarf. When she was in the fields, she let it down to brush and comb it. It shone like gold in the sunshine. Curdken crept up behind her and tried to pull some of it out.

So the princess began to sing a little song:

"*Blow, breezes, blow,*
Make Curdken's hat go!
Let him chase it all day,
Blow it far, far away!"

The wind blew Curdken's hat off his head. He had to chase it over the fields and hills. When he got back, the princess's hair was safely tied up in her scarf.

This happened again the next day.

The princess spoke to the horse as she
went through the gate:

*"Falada, poor Falada, hanging up
there!"*

The horse answered:

>"Princess, poor princess, passing
>>down there!
>Alas, alas, if your mother knew,
>How sad her heart would be for
>>you!"

When they were out in the fields with the geese, the princess shook out her golden hair and sang her little song:

"Blow, breezes, blow,
Make Curdken's hat go!
Let him chase it all day,
Blow it far, far away!"

Curdken's hat blew away again. He ran after it, and when he got back, the princess's hair was tied up again.

HARRISON DISTRICT 2
STRATTON MEADOWS

This time Curdken was so cross, he went to tell the king about it. "That new goose girl talks to a horse's head," he said. "And it answers her. And then she makes my hat blow away! I think she's a witch!"

On the third day, the king decided to follow them, to see what happened.

He heard the goose girl say to the horse:
"Falada, poor Falada, hanging up there!"

He heard the horse answer:

"*Princess, poor princess, passing*
down there!
Alas, alas, if your mother knew,
How sad her heart would be for
you!"

Then the king hid behind a bush and
watched the goose girl comb her hair. He
knew that only a princess could have such
beautiful golden locks. She sang:

"Blow, breezes, blow,
Make Curdken's hat go!
Let him chase it all day,
Blow it far, far away!"

When Curdken ran after his hat, the king came out from behind the bush. "Tell me who you are!" he said.

"I dare not!" sobbed the princess. "I promised, by the sky above, not to tell a living person. She'll kill me if I do!"

The king followed her home to a poor cottage. In it there was a big iron stove for burning wood.

"If you won't tell me," he said, "whisper it to the old stove. That is not a living person."

The poor princess was crying. She longed to tell her sorrows to somebody, but a princess never breaks a promise. So she crept up to the old stove.

"Here I am, alone, with no friends," she whispered. "I am a princess and my maid has taken my place with the prince. I have to wear rags and look after the geese. If my mother the queen knew it, her heart would break."

Now the old king was standing just outside the cottage. He could hear all that the princess said, through the stove-pipe in the wall.

That night he gave a great feast at the palace. Everybody was invited. The false princess sat with the young prince at one end of the long table. The king and the

real princess sat at the other end. She wore a gold and silver dress and looked lovely. Everybody wondered who she was. Nobody, not even the maid, guessed that she was the goose girl.

After they had eaten, the king told a story about a servant who had pretended to be his master.

"How do you think he should be punished?" he asked the false princess.

"Take away all his fine clothes and put him in a barrel. Have two horses drag it through the streets. Then turn him out of town!" said the maid, with a wicked laugh.

"What a good idea!" said the king. "That shall be *your* punishment!"

So the false princess was turned out of the town, and she was never heard of again.

Everybody was pleased with the real princess. She was so beautiful and gentle. The young prince married his true bride, and they ruled their kingdom together in peace and happiness.